10.70d

The Teacher
from the
Black Lagoon

by Mike Thaler · pictures by Jared Lee

SCHOLASTIC INC.

New York Toronto London Auckland Sydney

For Dr. Jerry Weiss,
who loves books
and kids
—M.T.

To all my teachers
at the now defunct
Van Buren High School
—J.L.

3317893

ISBN 0-590-41962-5

35   0 1 2/0

Printed in the U.S.A.   23
First Scholastic printing, October 1989

It's the first day of school.
I wonder who my teacher is.

I hear Mr. Smith has dandruff and warts,

and Mrs. Jones has a whip and a wig.

But Mrs. Green is supposed to be a *real* monster.
Oh my, I have *her*!
Mrs. Green...room 109.
What a bummer!

I sit at a desk.
I fold my hands.
I close my eyes.
I'm too young to die.

Suddenly a shadow covers the door.
It opens....

In slithers Mrs. Green.
She's *really* green!

She has a tail.
She scratches her name on the blackboard—with her claws!

Freddy Jones throws a spitball.

She curls her lip and breathes fire at him.
Freddy's gone.

There is just a little pile of ashes on his desk.

"Talk about bad breath," giggles Eric Porter.

She slithers over, unscrews his head,
and puts it on the globe stand.

I bet she gives homework the first day of school.

"Your homework for today," grins Mrs. Green,
smoke rising from her nostrils,
"is pages 1 to 200 in your math book—
all the fraction problems."

"We've never had fractions," shouts Derek Bloom.
"Come up here," she beckons with her claw.

Derek stands by her desk.
"This is a whole boy," she smirks.

She takes a big bite.
"This is half a boy. Now you've had fractions."

Doris Foodle cracks her gum.

Mrs. Green swallows her in one gulp!
"No chewing in class," she smiles.

Mr. Bender, the principal, sticks his head in.
"Keep up the good work,"
he nods and closes the door.
I wish I could get sent to the principal's office.

"Let's call the roll," cackles Mrs. Green.
"Freddy Jones is absent.
Derek Bloom is half here.
Eric Porter is here and there.
Doris Foodle is digesting."

"What about spelling?" shouts Randy Potts.
"Spelling can be *fun*!" beams Mrs. Green,
wiggling her fingers at him.

"Abracadabra Kazam!"
"That's tough to spell," says Randy.
Suddenly there's a flash of light, a puff of smoke,
and Randy's a frog.

Penny Weber raises her hand.
"Can I go to the nurse?" she whines.
"What's wrong?" asks Mrs. Green.
"I have a huge headache," says Penny.

Mrs. Green wriggles her fingers. There's another flash of light, and Penny's head is the size of a pin.

"Better?" asks Mrs. Green.

"Now it's naptime. Everyone who still has one, put your head on your desk."

I hope I make it to recess.

"Sweet dreams," she cackles as I close my eyes.

Suddenly the bell rings.
I wake up.
There's a pretty woman writing her name
on the blackboard.

She has real skin and no tail.
"I'm Mrs. Green, your teacher," she smiles.

I jump out of my chair, run up, and hug her.

"Well, thank you," she says,
"I'm glad to be here."

Not as glad as I am!